ROSELLE PUBLIC LIBRARY
3 3012 00367 4252

P9-BYZ-408

V

In memory of Emma Gargiulo Ortiz

ISBN 978-0-545-41584-2

I Spy Letters was originally published as a board book
under the title *I Spy Little Letters.*

28 27 26 25 24 23 22 21 17

Printed in the U.S.A. 40 • This edition first printing, January 2012

I SPY LETTERS

Rhymes by Jean Marzollo
Photographs by Walter Wick

Cartwheel BOOKS®

SCHOLASTIC INC.
New York Toronto London Auckland
Sydney Mexico City New Delhi Hong Kong

I spy letters

on a big red ,

an airplane ,

and an ant 

that's crawling away.

A C
E F
J K
H
P
M
N T U V
Q R S
Y Z
W X

I spy balloons
on the letter B,
and snow white ice
on an ice cold C.

B
C

I spy dots

on the letter D,

a nice soft

pi raser E.

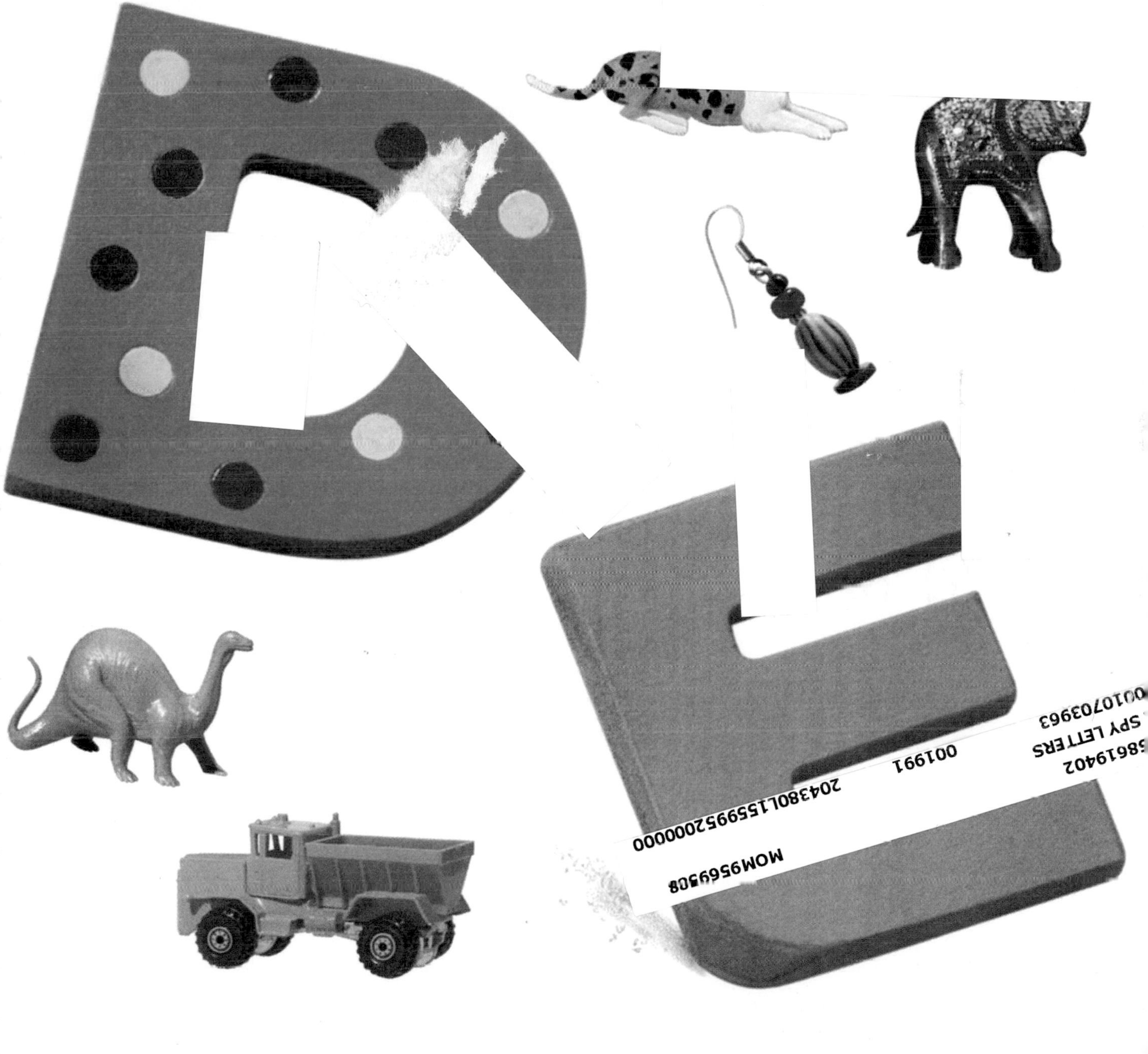
SPY LETTERS

I spy fire on an F

for me,

and golden glitter

on the letter G.

I spy holes in an 

that's green,

and inches on a ruler.

Do you see what  mean?

1
MADE IN U.S.A
2
NO. R 501-12
3
4

I spy jewels

on the letter J,

and bright red kites

on the letter K.

I spy an L
wearing lacy white,
and a metal M
that's screwed on tight.

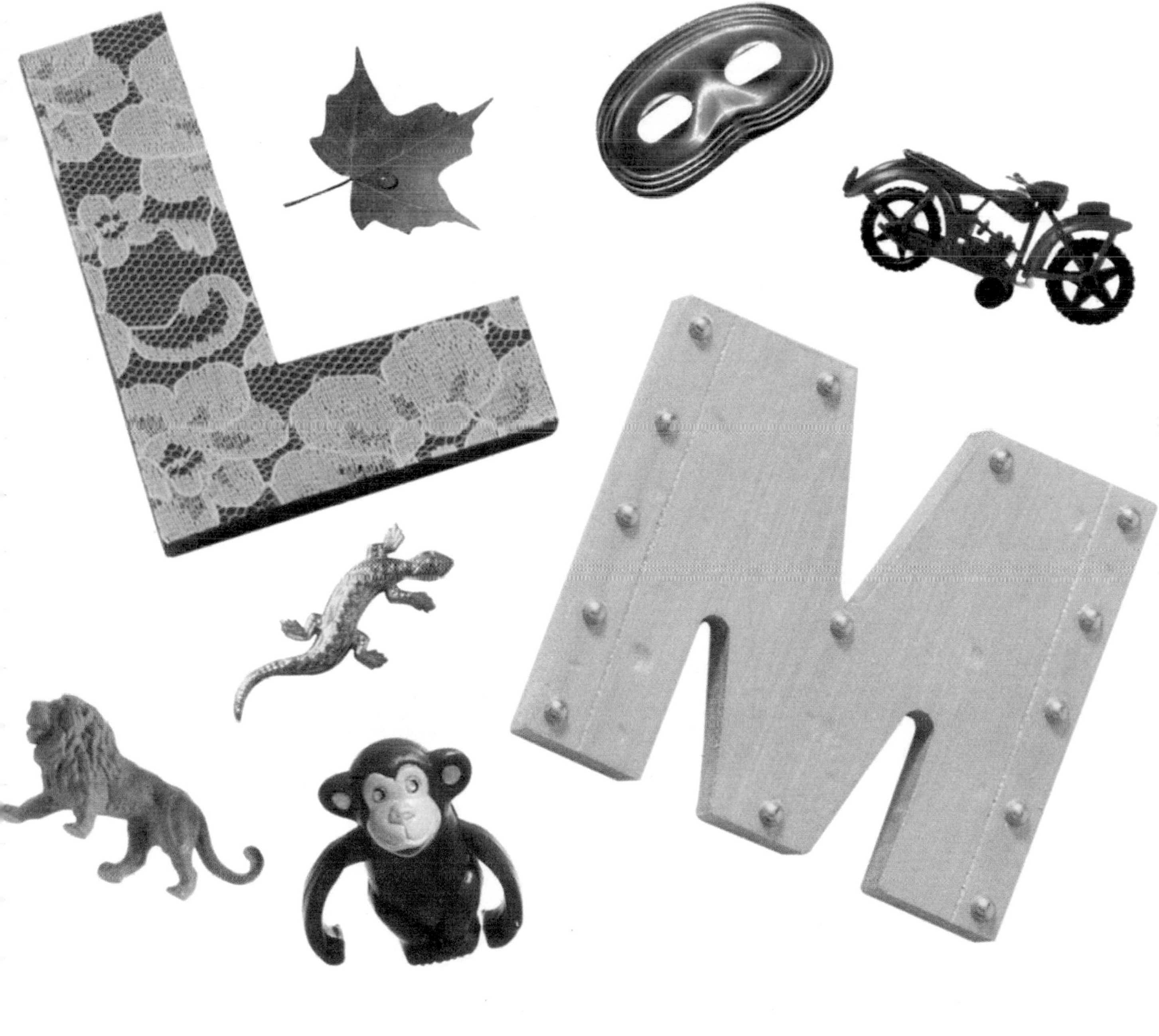

I spy an 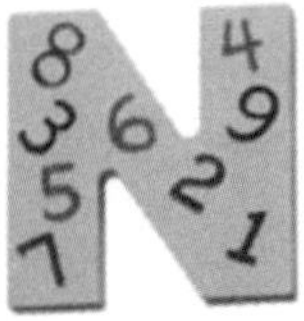

with numbers 1 to 9,

and an orange 

that's oh-so-fine.

I spy a red plaid
letter P,
and a question mark Q
for you and me.

I spy a rough
and rocky 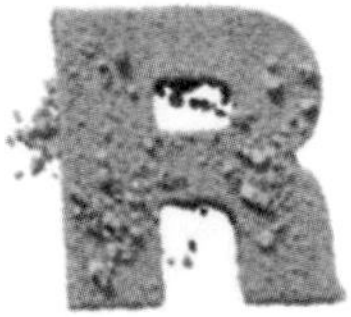,
a sky-blue ,
and a yellow star .

I spy a T

with triangles, too,

and a UFO

on a universal U.

T
U

I spy vines
on the letter V,
and a wet W
with a watery sea.

A Valentine

I spy an X, a Y,

two Zs;

Can you sing your

ABCs?

Exit

Collect the I Spy books

Classics

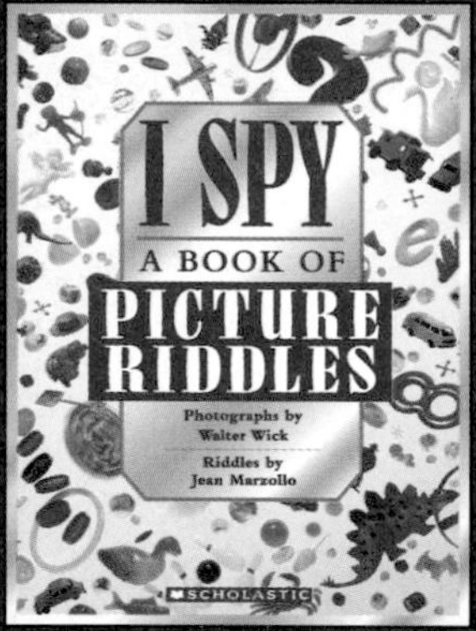

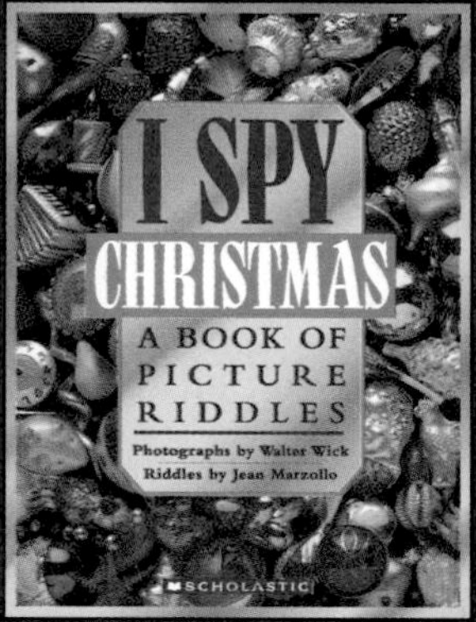

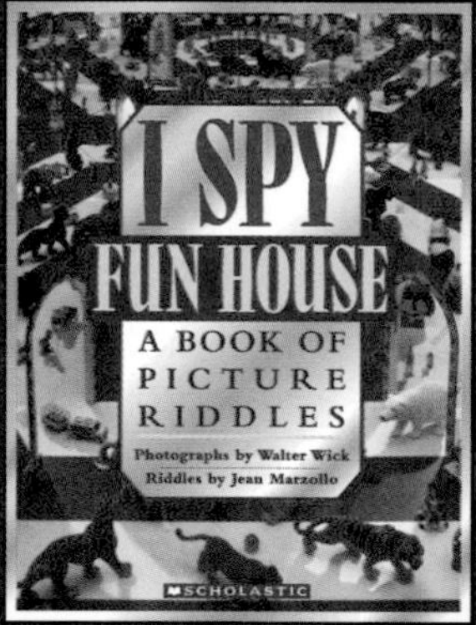

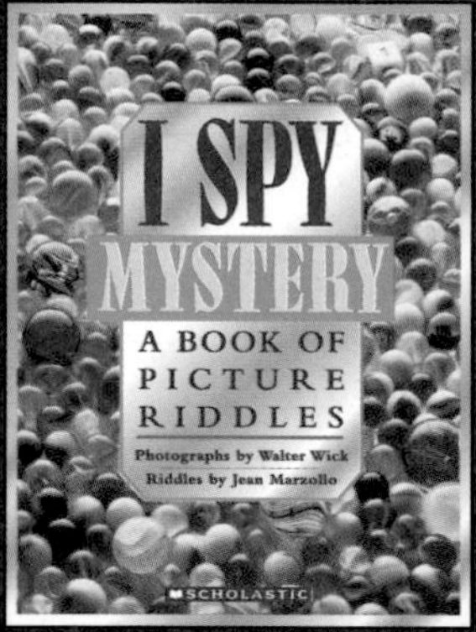

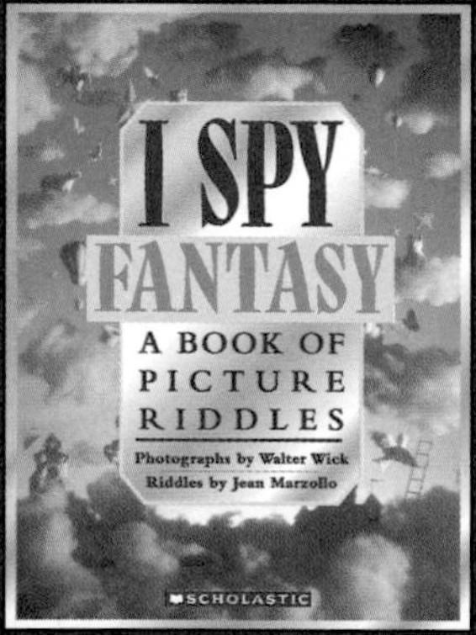

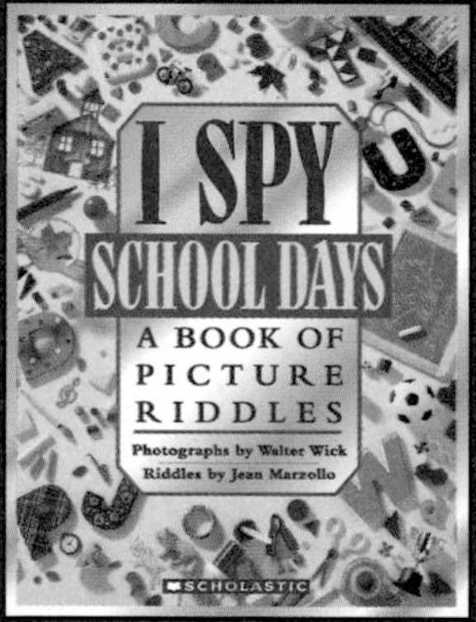

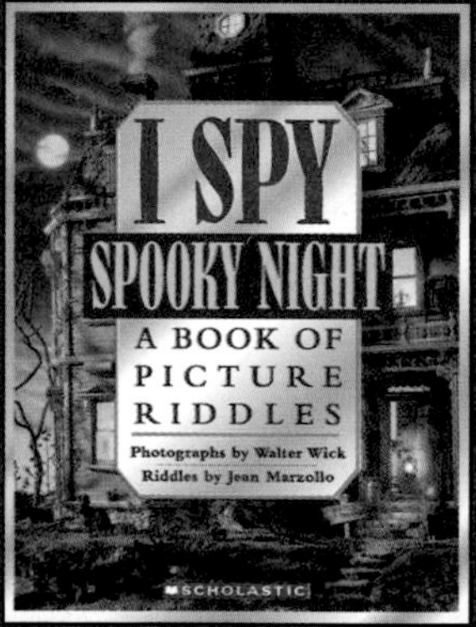

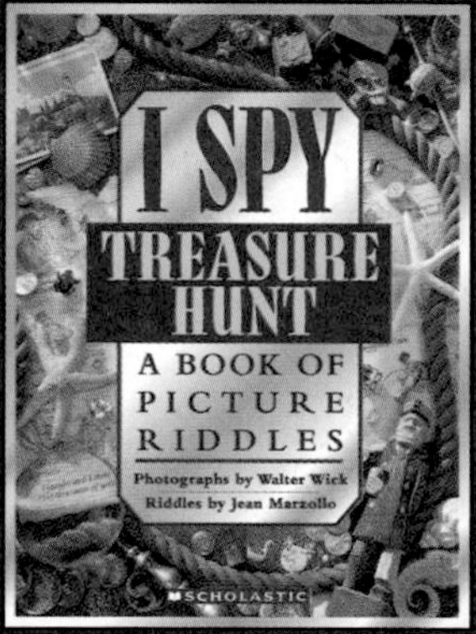

Collect the I Spy books

Challengers

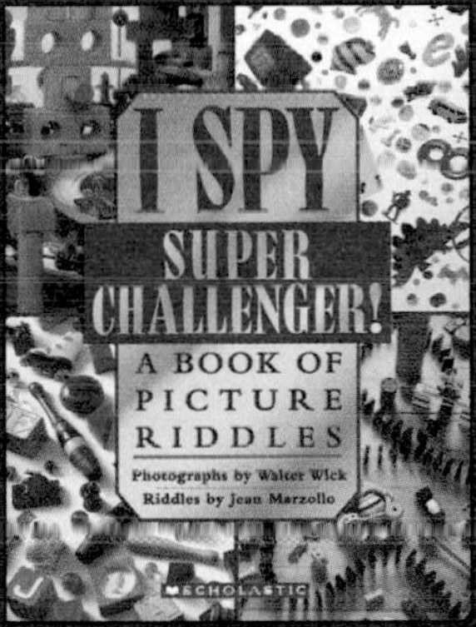

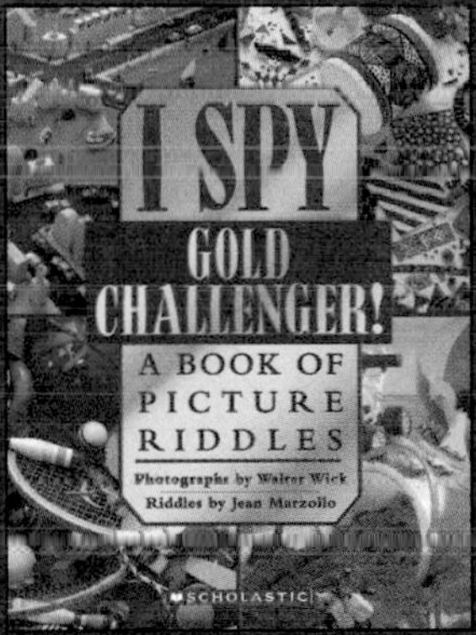

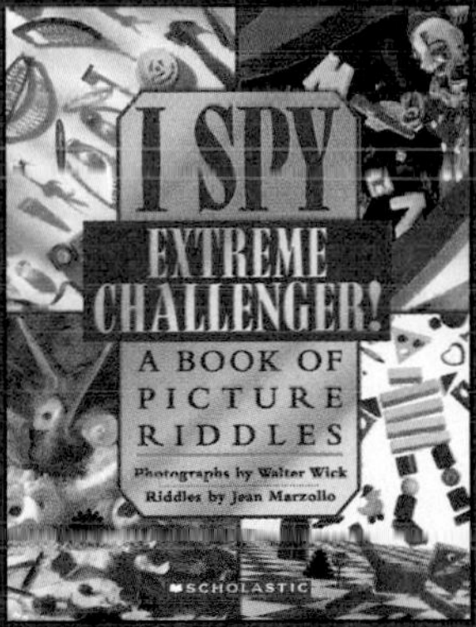

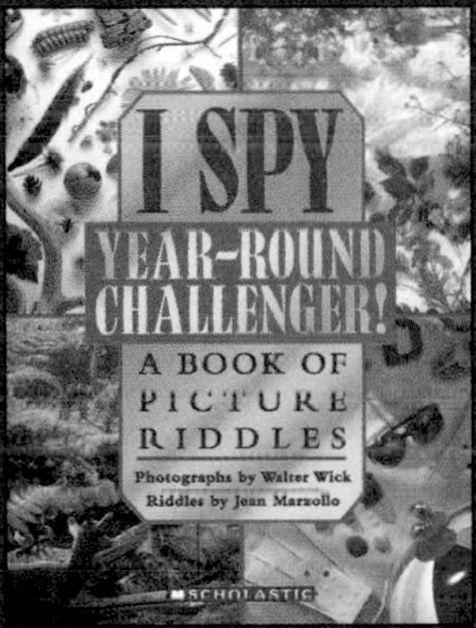

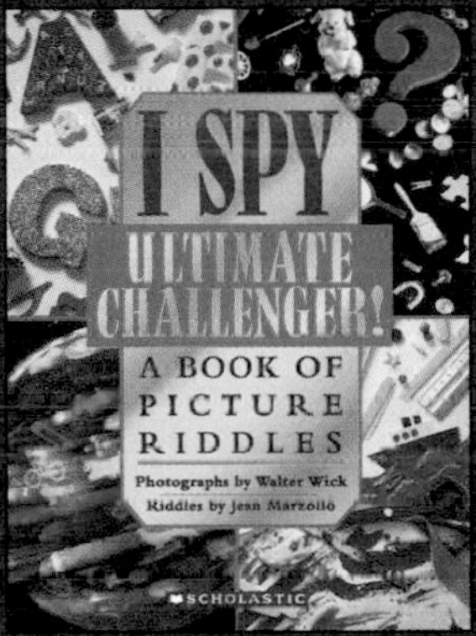

Also available are *I Spy A to Z*, *I Spy Spectacular*, I Spy early readers, I Spy Little board books, and *I Spy Phonics Fun*.

Find all the I Spy books and more at www.scholastic.com/ispy/.